For my mother and father
Alison

For Rebecca (Baby Ginger)
Aunty Cathy

First published in Great Britain in 2001
by Egmont Books Limited,
239 Kensington High Street, London W8 6SA.

Text copyright © Alison Ritchie 2001
Illustrations copyright © Cathy Gale 2001
The author and illustrator have asserted their moral rights

ISBN 0 7497 4661 0

A CIP catalogue record for this title is available from the British Library

Printed in UAE

1 3 5 7 9 10 8 6 4 2

I Don't Want to Sleep ALONE!

Alison Ritchie

illustrated by **Cathy Gale**

EGMONT

Mummy and Daddy had a big bed.
They slept in it together.

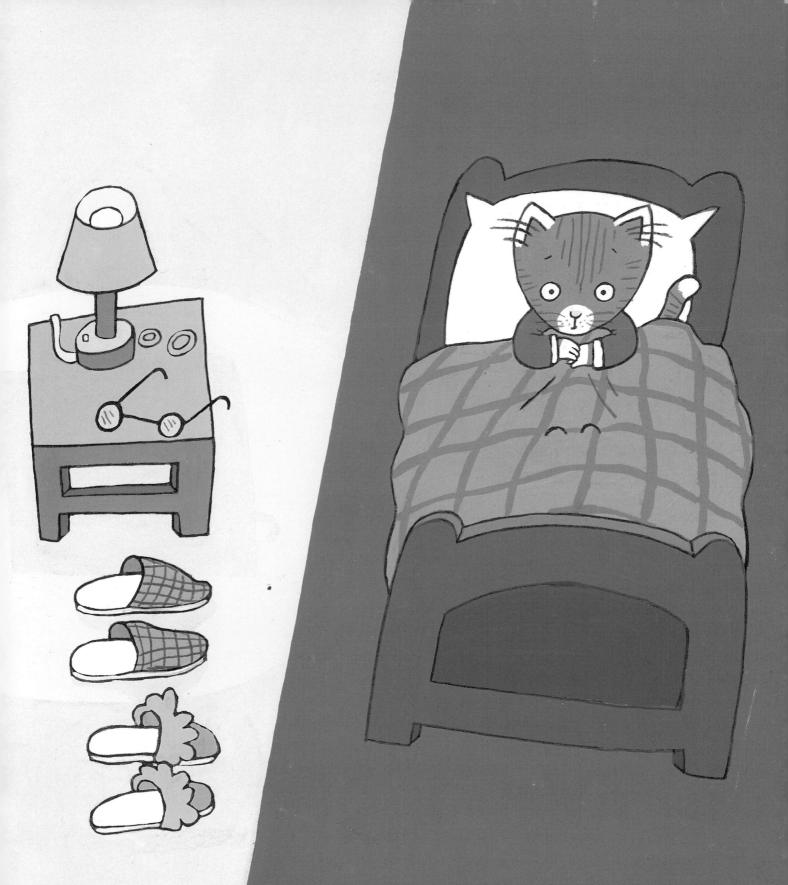

Joey had his own little bed.
He hardly slept in it at all.

At bedtime, he had a bath, brushed his teeth, and listened to **three** stories.

He kissed Mummy
goodnight,

he kissed Daddy
goodnight,

and he fell asleep.

But in the middle of the night, he woke up.

"I'm all alone!" he thought.

"I don't like it!"

So he climbed out of bed and crept into Mummy and Daddy's room. He crawled under the duvet and snuggled up beside them.

He squiggled and wriggled.

His paws poked into Daddy's back.
His whiskers tickled Mummy's face.

The next morning, Mummy was squashed up
against Daddy, and Daddy was hanging off
the edge of the bed.

"**Joey!**" said Mummy.
"You must stay in your **own** bed! There just isn't
room for **everybody** in our bed."

"It's not fair!" said Joey.

"You and Daddy are grown-ups, and you don't sleep alone. I'm only little, and I have to be **all by myself."**

That night, Mummy gave Joey his favourite teddy.
"He'll look after you," she said.
Joey hugged Mummy and Daddy goodnight and
cuddled Teddy.
Then he fell asleep.

But in the middle of
the night, Joey woke up.

He went to Mummy and Daddy's room.

The next morning, Daddy was cross. "What happened to Teddy?" he said.

"Teddy squiggled and wriggled all night long," said Joey.

That night, Daddy gave Joey his **cuddly bunny.**
"Bunny won't budge," he said. "He's a very
good bunny!"
Joey fell asleep . . .

. . . **but** in the middle of the night,
he crept into Mummy and Daddy's room.

"Bunny kept **poking me** in the back!" he said.

"How about **Monkey?**" said Mummy
and Daddy wearily.

But in the middle of the night . . .

"Monkey kept **tickling me** in the face."

The next night everyone was very tired.
"What about cuddling **Elephant**
tonight?" said Daddy.

But . . .

. . . in the middle of the night . . .

"Elephant was **squashing me.**"

The next night everyone went to bed very early.
"This is **Donkey**," said Mummy. "I've had
him since I was as little as you. Maybe he
can help you sleep."
Joey snuggled down with Donkey.

But in the middle of the night . . .

"Donkey kicked me right out of bed!"

"RIGHT!

That's it!"

said Mummy and Daddy.

"You've tried Teddy,
Bunny,
Monkey,
Elephant
and Donkey.

We've run out of toys, Joey –
what shall we do
NOW?"

"**Nothing,**" said Joey with a **big** yawn.
"There just isn't room for **everybody** in my bed."

"I want to sleep
ALONE!"

And he slept soundly in his **own** bed
all night long.

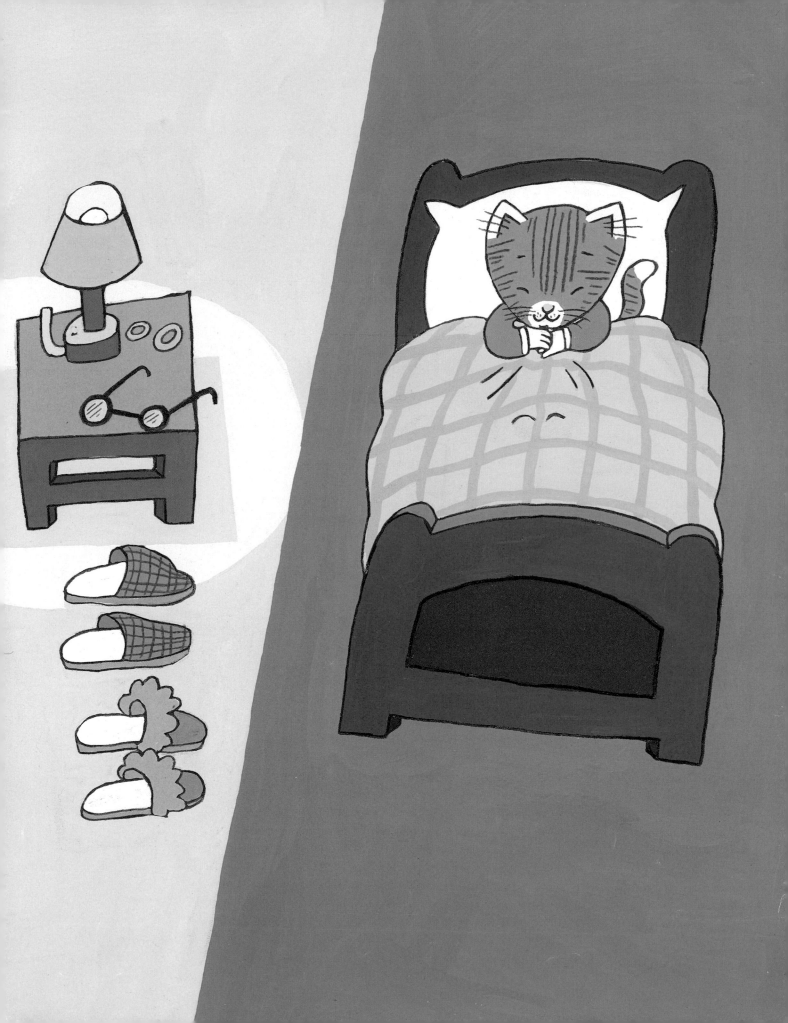

Koala and the Flower by Mary Murphy
0 7497 4407 3

A Story for Hippo
by Simon Puttock and Alison Bartlett
0 7497 4022 1

Mr Wolf's Pancakes by Jan Fearnley
0 7497 3559 7

Cat's Colours by Jane Cabrera
0 7497 3120 6

Dog's Day by Jane Cabrera
0 7497 4392 1

I wish I were a dog by Lydia Monks
0 7497 3803 0

The Three Little Wolves and the Big Bad Pig
by Eugene Trivizas and Helen Oxenbury
0 7497 2505 2

And they're all only £4.99